MATTY LONG

SUPER HAPPY MAGIC FOREST

AND THE PORTALS OF PANIC

OXFORD
UNIVERSITY PRESS

THE SUPER HAPPY HEROES

Hoofius (faun)

A delightful mix of pointy and furry bits, Hoofius likes to take on the role of leader of the heroes. He takes questing very seriously and holds nothing but contempt for clothes and personal grooming.

Blossom (unicorn)

A champion frolicker, Blossom is impulsive and likes to live in the moment. His unpredictable nature surprises friends and enemies alike.

He also eats like a horse.

Twinkle (fairy)

The only airborne member of the group, Twinkle is a useful scout and surprisingly strong for her size. She's also easily distracted by anything cute or shiny.

Herbert (gnome)

Rake-wielder and packer of picnics. Questing without Herbert would likely see you lost, hungry, and unable to identify wild flowers.

Trevor (mushroom)

Small, squishy, and great in an omelette; what Trevor lacks in size and limbs, he makes up for in smart ideas and sharp one-liners.

CHAPTER ONE
THE BEAST FROM BEYOND

It all happened on a morning, just like any other, in the SUPER HAPPY MAGIC FOREST. Giant candy sticks shone in the sunlight as butterflies danced through flowerbeds. Gnomes fished. Fairies fluttered. Pixies played games of hide-and-seek that would sometimes go on for hours, or days. Unicorns frolicked in the meadows to the sound of pan pipes and birds singing in the trees. There was so much to see, and even more to do . . .

What started suddenly as a small ripple in
the air . . .

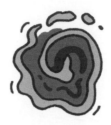

. . . soon became a dark hole, large enough
to disappear into, if you weren't careful.

It started to crackle, lit up by bolts of lightning from deep within.

The hole was getting harder to ignore.

But as soon as it had fully formed, it began to shrink.

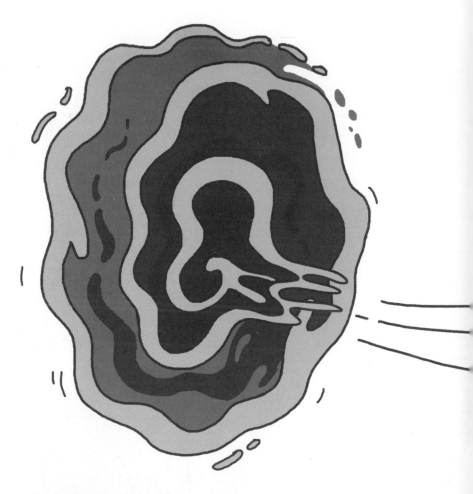

And just before it totally vanished . . .

A flappy blur of claws and teeth lashed out at the panicked onlookers, who started to run for cover.

Ice creams were wrenched from hooves.

Lollipops were plucked from mouths.

Candy floss was taken from babies.

No sweet treat was safe within the whirlwind of sticky destruction.

After the beast had gulped down the last morsel, its huge wide eyes looked frantically around for the next bite.

'That thing will eat its way through the whole forest!' cried one pixie. 'To the candy floss cave! Protect it with your lives!'

But the beast had caught the scent of something else. Its nose twitched, as a mouthwatering treat beckoned. It beat its wings and took to the air in search of the smell.

Meanwhile, in a cottage nearby two gnomes sat down to breakfast.

'I haven't baked waffles for years!' said Gnomedalf, as he ambled from the kitchen, his trademark broom in one hand and a full plate in the other. The aroma filled the room and drifted out of the open window. His guest was Herbert, a younger gnome who had made a name for himself as something of a heroic adventurer, though dolloping berries and cream on to fresh waffles was Herbert's only quest for this morning. Or at least, that's what he thought.

Something flashed through the window and the breakfast table erupted before Herbert's eyes. A creature was thrashing around, gobbling waffles and ignoring any idea of table manners. It was Herbert who ended up covered in berries and cream.

'Shoo! Away with you! I know how to use this!'

Gnomedalf was swinging his broom at the beast, like a gnome possessed.

Eat brush, scoundrel!

Herbert grabbed the last waffle and
slowly backed towards a cupboard, opening
the door and flinging the waffle inside.
The beast leapt in after it and Herbert
slammed the door shut, trapping it.

'What's going on in there?' huffed the
unmistakable voice of Tiddlywink the Pixie.
He and the rest of The Council of Happiness
(a group that deals with all the big forest
matters) were stood outside, where a
crowd had started to gather.

This better be
important! I'm
missing my
pottery class!

'Everything is under control!' said Herbert, as a chunk of cream dripped from his nose onto the ground. Tiddlywink's eyes narrowed in suspicion.

The rest of Herbert's questing group—fondly known by all as The Heroes—had also arrived at the scene.

Twinkle the fairy had seen the mayhem unfold and rounded up Blossom the unicorn, Hoofius the faun, and Trevor the mushroom straight away.

Blossom immediately set about helping to clear up the mess.

Stop that!

Tiddlywink was running out of patience.

'We're hearing reports of candy-based-carnage! Winged beasts! Swirling black holes! What in the name of cheesecake is going on here?'

'You'd best come in, councillors,' said Gnomedalf. 'And you too!' he added, pointing at the heroes. 'I fear something foul is afoot.'

They entered his cottage and closed the door.

Oh, I guess we're not invited.

Typical.

'. . . and so now the beast is locked in the cupboard.' Gnomedalf finished filling everyone in on his breakfast nightmare.

Trevor glanced at the cupboard and then at Herbert, still covered in cream.

'Is this how you treat all your breakfast guests?' joked the mushroom.

Tiddlywink walked over and pressed his ear to the door. 'Are you sure it's in here? I don't hear anything.' He opened the door a crack to peek inside.

The kitchen descended into chaos.

Trying to escape, the panicked beast ducked and dived among them, finally coming to a halt on one of Gnomedalf's hanging saucepans.

It fell to the ground, out cold. They all gathered around.

'THAT'S IT!?' cried Tiddlywink. 'This flying gremlin thing is the cause of all this hullabaloo?'

'I fear this is no mere gremlin,' sighed Gnomedalf, using the handle of his broom to examine the creature. 'If this is what I *think* it is, then we could all be in great danger.'

CHAPTER TWO
OFF TO SEE THE WIZARDS

'A por-WHAT?' asked Tiddlywink, as Gnomedalf poured ten cups of hugberry tea.

'A *PORTAL*,' said Gnomedalf, who had barely had a chance to speak before the pixie started butting in. 'It's like a magical door to a different place, or even world,' he continued. 'I suspect that this creature travelled from its own world to ours through a portal that was opened above the Super Happy Magic Forest.'

'What kind of different world?' asked Butterfly Horse nervously.

'One of darkness and shadow that is home to foul beasts like this.' Gnomedalf motioned to the creature on the floor. It was curled up and snoring softly.

Awww. It's kind of cute.

'Ha! A foul shadow beast indeed!' laughed Tiddlywink. 'What will it do next—drool on the carpet? Ha ha!'

'THIS IS NO LAUGHING MATTER!' boomed Gnomedalf, and Tiddlywink shrank back in his chair. 'This one alone was enough to terrorize our forest! What if more appear? Even bigger monsters? We don't have saucepans large enough to fight off such untold horror.'

The room fell silent, apart from the scratching of Admin Bunny's pencil, as she scribbled everything down.

Beasts...
...saucepans...
...untold horror.
Got it!

'But how did the portal open?' asked Sunshine.

'Portals are opened by magic. Only *wizards* can cast such powerful spells,' replied Gnomedalf. He turned to the five heroes. 'Once again, I fear that the Super Happy Magic Forest needs your help. Take the beast to Wizard City and find Barnabus Five-hats. He is the wisest wizard there is. He should know what to do.'

'Hold on a minute! The Council of Happiness dishes out the quests around here!' interrupted Tiddlywink. 'And I say that YOU should go with them!'

Gnomedalf's face fell. 'Me? But . . . but . . . why?'

'Because you seem to know a lot about all this wizard business!'

'Hooray!' cried Butterfly Horse. 'A new hero! How exciting!'

Admin Bunny handed Gnomedalf a sheet. 'Please fill out Hero Form 7C. Be sure to tick the box that says the Council of Happiness won't be blamed for any bad stuff that happens to you on the quest.'

That doesn't seem fair.

Wait till you hear about the joining fee.

With the paperwork signed, all that remained was for Herbert to pack for the quest.

Hmm. Which fishing rod should I take?

Hurry up, Herbert!

Eventually, the heroes were all together on the road to Wizard City. *Almost*.

Wait for me!

But the beast didn't seem as keen as
Herbert on going with them. Hoofius gave
its leash a strong yank. *That* got it moving.

Oww!

Well. Now
you're even.

'Try being more friendly,' urged Twinkle.

She rummaged in Herbert's backpack and
pulled out a waffle, tearing off a chunk.
The beast let go of Hoofius and gobbled it
down.

'I think we should give it a name,' said
Twinkle.

'How about . . . DORIS?' suggested Blossom, who clearly hadn't given it much thought.

'I think I'll call him . . . *Chompy*,' Twinkle said, as the beast sank its teeth into the last bite.

The journey went more smoothly from then on. Chompy seemed much happier to be led by Twinkle, and the road found some of the heroes in fine voice.

Gnomedalf, however, had kept quiet all the way. Until now.

'Oh dear! I'm afraid I'm too old for such a journey . . . my legs aren't what they were! I'll only slow you down. Go on without me!'

'Uh-oh. Somebody wants a piggyback,' joked Trevor.

Gnomes are hardy folk, and most remain very active right up until the oldest age. They all looked at Gnomedalf suspiciously.

'Besides, cities are no place for an old gnome like me!' he continued. 'Too busy! Too dirty! I'll be no help to you when I get lost or poorly! Oh! And who will judge the biggest carrot competition while I'm gone? Did anyone think about the carrots?

I must return!

'Why don't we talk about it over lunch?' suggested Herbert.

They had been walking along a forest path that opened into a sunlit glade.

It was prime picnic territory.

As Chompy had been as good as gold, Twinkle rewarded him with a waffle. But the good behaviour wasn't to last. After he'd finished his appetizer, Chompy was ready for a main course.

'Aw cute! He wants to eat you,' said Twinkle, as Hoofius tried to wrench their mushroom friend out of Chompy's mouth. When he finally let go, they all gasped.

'Trevor, are you OK?' asked Twinkle.

I think so. Though I feel a bit light-headed.

They didn't have the heart to tell Trevor that this might be because part of his head was sitting in Chompy's belly. It would probably grow back, anyway.

The heroes settled back down for their picnic, with Chompy tied to a tree and safely away from anything he might bite or pull.

It was only when the paper plates came out that they realized.

Gnomedalf had disappeared.

They scanned the glade for signs of the gnome.

But Gnomedalf really was nowhere to be seen.

CHAPTER THREE

ROYAL DISAPPROVAL

G nomes aren't natural runners, but Gnomedalf was giving it good go. *I can't go to Wizard City! I'll never make it out!* he thought, charging away from the others and back the way they came. At least, he *thought* he was going back, but he must have taken a wrong turn somewhere, because, suddenly, the path ended at the edge of a cliff.

And Gnomedalf didn't stop in time . . .

Twinkle hauled Gnomedalf back to safety, and helped the rather shaken old gnome back to the picnic where the other heroes welcomed him warmly. But it wasn't long until questions were asked.

'You're hiding something, aren't you?' said Hoofius. 'What's going on here? Why are you so scared of Wizard City?'

Gnomedalf sighed. There was no getting out of this one now. He had to see the quest through. And that meant his companions needed to know the truth. He took a deep breath, and began to spill the beans. 'I was once a great wizard. Gnomedalf Four-hats was my name, and I sat on the Wizard City Council.'

'You? *Gnomedalf? A wizard?*' I never would have guessed!' said a clearly impressed Herbert.

Gnomedalf continued. 'But my time in Wizard City came to a sudden end when I was . . . BANISHED.'

Ooooh, this is getting good!

'It was the day of The Great Wizard Bake-tacular. It's a *very* serious baking competition, with absolutely NO MAGIC ALLOWED. However, I was disqualified for using an enchanted rolling pin. But I have no idea how that happened!'

THE ROLLING PIN OF SHAME

'They stamped on my hats and snapped my wizard staff in two, so that I couldn't perform any magic again. They then banished me from the city and said that if I ever went back they would lock me up in wizard prison. FOREVER.

'That's why I just tried to run away. I am afraid of what will happen if I get caught. After finding a home in the Super Happy Magic Forest, it would devastate me to never see it again.'

'But by coming with us, you can help protect it!' said Hoofius, his fist in the air. 'You don't need to worry. We'll finish this quest together! Together, we . . .'

His voice trailed off. There was a noisy commotion nearby, and it was getting louder.

It was getting *closer.*

Voices. Movement. An unavoidable uproar was heading their way . . .

The heroes scrambled away as the picnic was ruined. Among the chaos the bigger beast locked eyes on the one thing that was barely moving—Chompy. It approached with teeth and claws at the ready.

'Hey! You have to get through ME FIRST!' yelled Twinkle.

As the beast was about to lash out, it suddenly stopped. Its skin hardened like a crust and there was an arrow stuck in its back. It had been turned to stone.

Three figures walked into the clearing. They were tall, with pointy ears and excellent dress sense, and they carried bows and arrows.

'My name is Nym, and we are wood elves,'
said the leader. 'You are now wandering
through the *Wood Elf Wood*.'

'We're still trying to think of a better name
for it,' added another elf.

Chompy stepped out from behind Twinkle
and Nym's eyes widened. The elves had
arrows pointed at Chompy before they
could blink.

'Please don't turn him to stone!' begged
Twinkle, trying to shield the creature.

Nym looked surprised. 'Why not? These
beasts have been rampaging through our
woods for days now, and more portals and
creatures are appearing across the land.
We don't know who or what is to blame.'

'Well that's what *we* intend to find out!' said Gnomedalf, warming to his role in the quest. 'So if you don't mind, we'll just be on our way . . .'

'Not gonna happen!' the elf said sharply. 'Our Queen would flip her lid if she found out we had let you go free. I'm afraid your future is in her hands now.'

The elves then led the group far from the path and through a maze of trees.

'Not the moose!' came a small voice. 'Ugh! Strawberry, move your noggin!'

'So what's going on here?' asked the Wood Elf Queen. 'It had better not be BORING.'

Nym told her everything, while acting out the most exciting moments with sound

45

effects to boot. When the performance was over, the Queen spoke.

'I can't let you walk off with *THAT* thing!' she said, pointing at Chompy. 'These monsters have to be stopped! What if they wanted to hurt my poor Strawberry?'

'But then, how will the wizards believe us with no proof?' pleaded Hoofius. 'Without their help the portals will keep opening and there will be *even more* monsters!'

'More ornaments for my garden,' said the Wood Elf Queen. 'I like to collect things. Nym! TURN THE BEAST TO STONE!'

'NOOOO!' cried Twinkle, as Nym let fly.

CHAPTER FOUR
BEARDUS THE CLEVER

The arrow shot towards Chompy as Twinkle gave his leash a strong yank, pulling him out of the way. It missed him by inches and disappeared into a thicket behind. Nym reached to her quiver for another arrow, but found it empty.

'We're out of stone arrows! We cannot hold off these beasts forever without them. Your Majesty, we have to let the prisoners all free to continue their quest and put an end to this chaos.'

47

The Queen frowned. Strawberry turned his head and whimpered as if trying to tell her something.

'OK, FINE. The monster can go free. BUT you *are* in my debt for being rescued. You owe me a favour and I WON'T forget it! Now go. I've got a moose to makeover.'

She brandished a hairbrush and some ribbons. 'Say goodbye to everyone, Strawberry.'

The moose groaned what might have been a cry for help, as Nym and her companions led the heroes out to the edge of the wood.

Sorry about that.
I hope Wizard
City gives you a
warmer welcome.

'I don't think we'll be going back *there* for a picnic,' said Herbert, as they continued their journey. He flicked through a Wizard City guidebook and entertained the others with facts about their destination as they walked.

'Fascinating. The more hats a wizard wears at one time, the more magic they have mastered!' he said.

'And the more problems they have walking through doorways,' added Gnomedalf.

Herbert opened up a map of the city, and the other heroes gathered around for a sneak peek at what lay ahead.

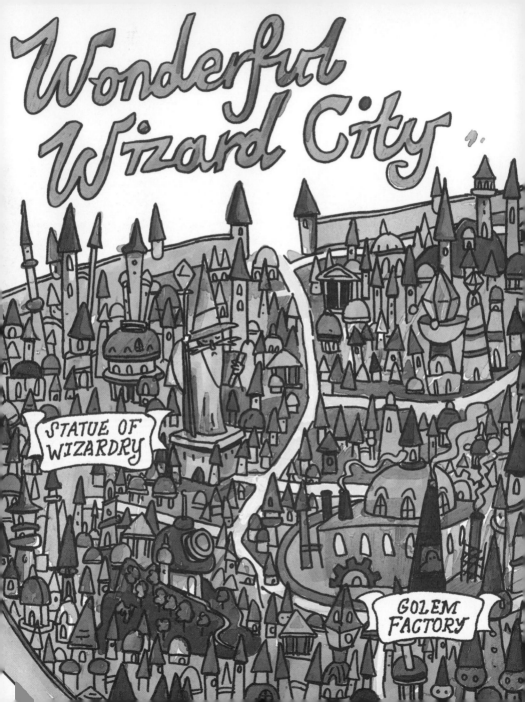

Note: This map is not to scale and famous landmarks have been enlarged for ease of use among tourists. Also, it took me a really really long time so I hope you like it. - Grand Cartographer Mattyus
GREAT LIBRARY
ARCANIUM
WIZARD PRISON

As they marvelled at the map, Gnomedalf slipped on a disguise.

'Blossom, that *is* Gnomedalf!' said Hoofius, restraining his friend.

'Not anymore!' the old gnome replied. 'From now on I am *Beardus the Clever*—the travelling wizard! And I think we may be close to our destination . . .'

They climbed a hill that revealed a skyline pierced by the towers of Wizard City.

'What are those golem things?' asked Hoofius.

'The guidebook says they're magical beings, created to help wizards with all sorts of jobs,' said Herbert.

'Indeed!' chimed Gnomedalf. 'My golem Betsy helped with all my chores. But I had to leave her behind. Who knows what became of her.' He sighed sadly at the thought, but then remembered the quest. 'We must hasten to the Arcanium. It's where the Grand Wizard Council sits and ponders matters of great importance like the meaning of life and what day the bins get collected.'

They followed Gnomedalf through wide,
clean avenues of white marble, topped
with shiny domes and spires.

'Look! the Statue of Wizardry!' said
Herbert, excitedly. 'It's very popular with
tourists.'

'And birds,' added Trevor.

'And over there is the Golem
Factory,' continued Herbert.
'I wonder if we'll have a
chance to pay it a visit . . .'

'Here we are!' called
Gnomedalf as the group
caught up to him.

SPELL

57

The Wizard's Council was in open session, and they joined a queue of those waiting to get their problem solved by the sharpest minds in the city.

As the queue shortened, Gnomedalf became more agitated. He looked around for any sign that his true identity had been uncovered. Under all that hair was one nervous gnome.

'Gnomedalf? Are you OK?' asked Blossom.

'Shhh! Remember: I am *Beardus the Clever*. Let me do the talking here. All going well, the wizards will take care of everything. Yes, everything will be just fine!'

The door opened and a golem appeared.

NEXT!

GOLEM, GOLEM, GONE

The great doors to the Wizard Council chamber opened, and the heroes stepped inside. Chompy crept behind them out of sight on Gnomedalf's order. He didn't want to cause any instant panic among the wizards without an explanation first.

The heroes were met with four sets of eyes looking down on them . . .

'Speak your business!' croaked the rather small and green Timothy Two-hats.

'Wow, you must be one smart frog!' observed Blossom.

'Not quite!' laughed Barnabus. 'You haven't mastered transformation magic, have you, Timothy?' The other wizards chuckled.

'He's still figuring out how to turn himself back into a human.'

'Please excuse Blossom,' said Gnomedalf. 'He shouldn't have spoken out of turn. Or AT ALL.' He turned and glared at the unicorn from behind his sunglasses.

'My name is Beardus the Clever. I am a travelling wizard and have definitely never been here or met you before.'

'Is that so?' said Barnabus, leaning closer.
'And who are you travelling with?'

'The fairy, faun, and gnome are my
apprentices. Blossom is my trusty steed
and the mushroom is . . . er . . . one of my
magic experiments!'

Trevor frowned as Barnabus peered at
him, noticing that a large chunk of his
head was missing.

'An unsuccessful experiment, I presume?'
Reminds me of the cake you attempted at
last year's Bake-tacular, Frederico!'
He burst into laughter.

There was
nothing wrong
with it!

'WIZARDS OF THE COUNCIL!' Gnomedalf boomed, snapping them back to attention. 'Portals are opening across the land, and monstrous creatures are emerging from them and causing havoc!'

The mood in the room changed in an instant. Barnabus's face dropped and Timothy let out an involuntary croak.

'Impossible!' said Frederico Four-hats, who had replaced Gnomedalf on the council after his banishment. 'Only a wizard with a summoning stone can open a portal. And the last summoning stone was destroyed by my great-grandfather Fredericus Five-hats—so that the creatures of darkness would never trouble this world again!'

There was a polite round of applause from the other three wizards in respect of Frederico's family legacy. Even Blossom gave him a clap, until a sharp elbow from Hoofius reminded him why they were there.

'Indeed!' said Barnabus. 'We have him to thank for a century of peace. If such monsters still troubled our world there would certainly be no time for our beloved baking competitions.'

The wizards nodded in agreement as Maggie Three-hats passed around a plate of jam tarts.

Ooh, plum jam! Maggie, you spoil me!

Gnomedalf sensed the moment was slipping away. 'Then how do you explain THIS?' he demanded, turning and pointing at Twinkle, who stepped aside, and the wizards laid eyes on Chompy for the first time. A gasp went up from the council.

'A portal creature? It . . . cannot be!' said Barnabus, dropping the tart in his lap. 'Oh dear, jam-side down. Frederico, would you inspect the beast?'

Frederico stood up and approached Chompy, fixing a monocle to his eye.

'Well?' urged Barnabus as he licked plum jam off his robes. Frederico turned his attention to the heroes, pausing for a moment on Gnomedalf, who seemed familiar, somehow. Frederico turned back to the council.

'Just as I suspected—a false alarm! I have studied portal creatures in great detail while researching my family's great history. I conclude that, while similar, this is just a gremlin and no more a portal beast than you or I!'

'Impossible!' cried Gnomedalf. 'We saw it fly from a portal with our own eyes. And there are more of them, too. We are all in danger!'

Twinkle suddenly felt Chompy's leash wrenched from her grip. Chompy leapt at the Wizard Council as they cried out in surprise.

Nooo! Not the tarts!

Maggie Three-hats scrambled for her wizard staff and, with a blast of magical energy, sent Chompy hurtling backwards into Gnomedalf, knocking him to the floor, and his sunglasses too.

'Gnomedalf?' said a shocked Barnabus.

IT'S HIM!

'Gnomedalf Four-hats, who used magic meddling in the Great Wizard Bake-tacular? Who was banished from Wizard City forever?'

Barnabus rose to his feet, his face a bit red. 'Trying to spoil another Bake-tacular with pretend portal beasts are you? Have another enchanted rolling pin up your sleeve as well, do you? GUARDS! Take him to . . . WIZARD PRISON!'

But Gnomedalf did not go quietly.

'Seek out the Great Library my friends!
Discover the truth! Don't worry about me!
Save the Super Happy Magic Forest!' he
called.

The heroes could only stand and watch as
the golems dragged Gnomedalf through
the doors and out of sight.

No! There's been a big mistake!

Sure has. There's not nearly enough jam in these tarts.

Oh dear.

CHAPTER SIX
SCRATCH AND SNIFF

The heroes found themselves back on the streets of Wizard City. Barnabus had advised Hoofius and the others to find new wizards to serve. Chompy was allowed to go with them. They had no use for a trouble-making gremlin.

It all added up to a quest that wasn't quite going to plan.

But Herbert was in no mood to wallow. 'We have no choice but to figure this out ourselves,' he said. 'And thanks to Gnomedalf, we know where to start. There must be a book that proves Chompy is a portal creature.'

He held out his arm for attention. 'TAXI!'

To the GREAT LIBRARY!

THUD
THUD

The front desk was staffed by a golem.

'I think this Golem's broken,' whispered Herbert.

They crept away and found a floor plan that detailed every subject in the library.

'Let's see here . . .' said the gnome. 'Baking . . . Botany . . . Street Dance. Ah–ha. Portal Magic!'

They scuttled up endless spiral staircases until they reached the Portal Magic section.

Er . . . Blossom?

Just . . . give me . . . a . . . . . . moment . . .

The room was gloomy, with a musty smell lingering between the bookshelves. Hoofius opened a window as the others began pulling out books.

'These books are so old,' said Herbert. 'The language is too complicated. I don't understand any of it.'

Twinkle offered him a book from high up on the top shelf. 'How about this?'

'*Portals for Dum-Dums*. Yes, this might be just what we need!'

They gathered around Herbert as he flicked through its pages, landing on what might be their golden ticket.

CREATURES of the PORTAL WORLD

LESSER GARGOYLE

- Smallest and weakest of the portal creatures
- Simple to summon through a portal due to small size
- Easily bullied and bossed around by bigger gargoyles
- Loves sweet treats and biting things

GREATER GARGOYLE

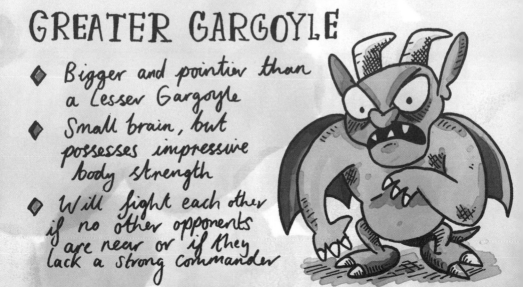

- Bigger and pointier than a Lesser Gargoyle
- Small brain, but possesses impressive body strength
- Will fight each other if no other opponents are near or if they lack a strong commander

MEGA GARGOYLE

- The biggest and most terrifying creature of the portal world
- Has an appetite for chaos and destruction
- Other gargoyles will obey its orders out of fear
- Only experts can summon and control them

A cold chill ran down their spines at the sight of the Mega Gargoyle. Except Trevor, of course. Mushrooms don't have spines.

'What if one of *those* comes through a portal?' said Hoofius. 'We'll all be doomed!'

As he spoke, the book rose into the air, floated towards the doorway, and into the hands of a wizard.

'Quite doomed,' agreed Frederico Four-hats, slamming the book shut. How long he had been there was anyone's guess.

Nobody had heard any footsteps echoing up the staircase.

'It seems you've spent too much time in the company of that fool, Gnomedalf,' said Frederico. 'Gargoyles only exist within the pages of dusty books like this. The summoning stones were all destroyed!'

'But . . . they can't have been if we have a gargoyle with us!' countered Hoofius.

'ENOUGH!' cried Frederico. 'I don't have time to listen to this nonsense. My great-grandfather Fredericus Five-hats was the greatest wizard that ever lived. You've seen the statue!'

'The one covered in poop?' said Trevor.

'Yes, that one! Made in his honour . . . for destroying the stones, and banishing the gargoyles forever. So I won't stand here and be questioned by a travelling circus of simpletons about matters of which they have no knowledge. There is a baking competition tomorrow, and I have much to prove. Begone from here!'

He waved the heroes away, as if swatting at flies.

'I think we'll stay,' said Herbert, defiantly. 'As the golems say, this is a library. And that means anyone is free to use it.'

'Oooh. Good comeback,' said Blossom, as the gnome settled himself on a footstool.

Frederico was about to scold Herbert like he would a useless apprentice, when he stopped at the sound of a scraping noise nearby.

They peered around the bookcase to see Chompy, scratching manically at the library wall. His eyes were wide, as if being drawn to a hidden power.

'That's weird. He's never done that before,' observed Hoofius.

'Oh, he's just . . . er . . . filing his nails on the wall,' declared Frederico, striding towards Chompy. 'It's classic *gremlin* behaviour. Nothing to see here!'

He leaned over to pick up the gargoyle, his beard dangling as he did so.

'Quite the lively fellow, isn't he?' said the clearly embarrassed wizard, after Twinkle had managed to pull Chompy away.

She giggled. 'You should see him after he's had ice cream.'

But Chompy hadn't finished yet. His nose twitched at the scent of something sweet that was wafting through the open window. It was irresistible.

'CHOMPY . . . NO!' cried Twinkle, as the beast struggled free of her grip.

He leapt through the open window and was gone.

Well, that's one way of avoiding the stairs.

CHAPTER SEVEN
THE GARGOYLE THIEF

'Wow, look at him go,' said Blossom, as the heroes watched Chompy spread his wings and glide towards the ground. Twinkle squeezed out of the window in hot pursuit.

'Go after them!' said Herbert to the others. 'I'll stay here and look for more clues.'

He braced himself for Frederico's opinions on the idea.

But the wizard was nowhere to be seen.

Hoofius, Blossom, and Trevor rushed down and out through the library, tempting the well-meaning wrath of many a golem along the way.

It didn't take them long to find the runaway gargoyle.

Twinkle grabbed Chompy's leash and pulled him away.

Whizzpop the wizard surveyed the carnage. 'Ah, man. That thing ate all my stock. And look at this mess! What a drag.'

'I'm SO sorry,' said Twinkle. 'I don't think they have manners where he's from.' She gave Chompy her best *you've been a very bad gargoyle haven't you?* face.

For once it looked as though he was actually sorry. Twinkle had tried to bring out the good in Chompy, even if he was a creature of darkness. Seeing him cower before the greater gargoyle had helped her realize that for all his beard-pulling, waffle-chomping, head-biting antics, he was still alone and far from home. Someone had to stick up for him.

Chompy let out a big waffle burp. *He really doesn't make it easy, though*, Twinkle thought, as she held her nose.

Blossom, meanwhile, was helping with the clean-up operation.

Blossom! Don't eat off the floor!

Yes. Put it on a plate first.

'These are DELICIOUS,' Blossom spluttered, spitting crumbs everywhere. 'They're the best ever!'

'There ain't no waffle like a Whizzpop Waffle. They're magic,' said the wizard. He clicked his fingers and a waffle appeared out of thin air, 'But . . . I can't make more waffles *and* clear up this mess! What's a wizard to do?'

'Let me help! I'll be a great waffle wagon worker!' said Blossom, who was practically trembling with excitement.

Hoofius groaned. 'I guess we do owe Whizzpop for all the damage Chompy caused. But you can only help out until we find out why all these portals keep appearing!'

Twinkle gave Blossom a hug. 'Thank you. And . . . try to do a good job.'

'You can count on me!' said the unicorn, licking his lips.

Hoofius, Twinkle, and Trevor made their way back to the Great Library. 'I never thought Blossom would be the first of us to get a job,' said Hoofius.

'He'll probably be the first to get fired from one too,' added Trevor.

Twinkle held Chompy's leash and let it trail behind her, as usual. He had sure been quiet. *Maybe I was too hard on him.*

She turned to check on the gargoyle, but there was nothing at the end of the leash.

'Over there!' cried Hoofius. Stomping away from them was a golem, holding Chompy tightly in its arms.

The three heroes bounded through busy streets, bumping into quite a few hapless wizards on the way and leaving a trail of magic-infused chaos in their wake.

But all they found was a grumpy golem-master, and they left the factory completely gargoyle-less. Twinkle was downbeat to say the least.

'I'm sorry. I should have taken better care of him,' she said sadly.

'It's not your fault,' said Hoofius. 'You're the best pet-gargoyle owner I've ever known! Besides, we can't give up yet. Chompy needs us, and we need him.'

'What about the others?' asked Trevor.

'They'll be fine!' said Hoofius. 'Blossom won't go far from the Waffle Wagon. And we left Herbert in the library.

What's the worst that could happen?'

CHAPTER EIGHT
GNOME ALONE

Herbert snored loudly, waking himself up. All around him lay big books on portal magic, none of which seemed helpful or could be considered light reading. You couldn't blame a gnome for nodding off.

If only Frederico hadn't taken *Portals for Dum Dums*, he thought.

So far Herbert had only been reading books within reach, and for a gnome that meant the bottom two shelves. So he began using his rake to prise books from higher up.

CLICK

He hooked a large book with his rake, and began to pull, but instead of falling, the book moved forward with a click. Herbert stumbled back in surprise, expecting to hit the wall behind him.

But the wall had vanished.

He had discovered a secret stairway.

His hand hovered where earlier Chompy had been scratching away at a solid wall. It was no illusion.

Herbert wondered if he should wait for his friends to return, but his curiosity got the better of him. He took his first nervous steps into the gloom.

He tiptoed up the stairs and into a dark room without windows. A glow was coming from a pedestal in the centre. A cloth was draped over it, as if there was something underneath that someone didn't want to be seen.

Herbert gave it a tug.

On top of the pedestal sat a stone, radiating with an unnatural energy.

Herbert jumped in surprise.

'This is it, Frederico! This is why gargoyles
have returned and are popping out
of portals!' said the gnome, almost
breathless at the discovery. 'It must have
been here all along, right under your
nose. We have to tell Barnabus at once!'

'Oh, Barnabus doesn't need to know about
this,' said the wizard, stepping closer. 'He'll
be too busy preparing for the contest
tomorrow. He'd hate to be disturbed.'

'Then . . . Maggie Three-hats?' Herbert
continued. 'Or . . . umm . . . what was the
name of the frog?'

Frederico loomed over Herbert, the glow
of the summoning stone revealing a
wicked grin on his face.

'On second thoughts . . . maybe I'll just be
on my way. Yes I—I'll just be leaving now!'
stammered the gnome, as realization took
hold, and he made a break for the stairs.

Herbert struggled against the magic, as his eyes widened at all the pictures and notes of portals and beasts that filled the walls.

'Impressive isn't it?' said Frederico. 'Not all my own work. My great-grandfather Fredericus deserves some credit, too.'

'But he destroyed all the summoning stones!' said Herbert, still bobbing up and down in the air.

'It was all an illusion,' cackled Frederico. 'He kept one stone hidden in this chamber, knowing it would be foolish to throw away such power. And now the day has come when it is needed. It shall be unleashed . . . at tomorrow's Great Wizard Bake-tacular!

Without their staffs, there will be no wizard to stop me from using this stone to summon . . .

A MEGA GARGOYLE!'

Hehehe!

'But why?' said Herbert, trying to stall the wizard in the hopes that his friends might return.

'Because . . .' began Frederico, but he was cut off by another voice within the room.

It was coming from a mirror on the wall, but it was no reflection. It wavered like a mirage.

MASTER! MASTER! PABLO CALLING!

'For goodness sake, Pablo, you're holding it upside down again!' said Frederico, turning back to Herbert. 'Honestly. Golems and modern technology . . .'

'MASTER. I HAVE SECURED THE LESSER GARGOYLE.'

'Excellent, Pablo. Please continue your household chores until further instruction.' As the vision faded and the mirror returned to normal, Frederico turned back to Herbert.

'It seems that your friends will be kept busy for quite some time. But time is exactly what they don't have! And as for you . . .'

The room began to ripple, and in front of Herbert a hole opened up in the air. He stared into it, and saw his fate.

'NOOOO!' He cried, as the portal sucked him in.

CHAPTER NINE
TOWER OF TERROR

It had been two hours since Twinkle, Hoofius, and Trevor had last seen Chompy being carried off by a mysterious golem. Twinkle had been flying amongst the roofs and tower tops scanning the streets below but it was no use. Chompy seemed long gone.

Until Trevor spotted a clue.

Are these pieces of Chompy's collar?

Twinkle found an open window halfway up the tower and squeezed through. A few tense moments passed before the front door unbolted and her head poked out. She beckoned them in.

'I don't think anyone's home,' she whispered, as they crept through the halls.

They searched every room on their way up.

Trevor! How do I look?

Confusing. Veeeery confusing.

They were starting to run out of rooms to check when they came to a closed door. Twinkle listened closely and heard a gnawing sound coming from the other side. She'd know that sound anywhere.

Twinkle tugged and pulled at the ropes that held the cage aloft as Hoofius and Trevor began looking for the key to unlock it.

And that's when Trevor found the mirror.

Trevor wasn't impressed. 'A gargoyle bit half my head off and nobody told me?'

'We thought it would grow back.' Hoofius shrugged. 'Besides, it makes you look tougher! More . . . battle-worn.'

Trevor turned back to the mirror to decide whether he *did* look tougher. But he got an even bigger fright than before.

Pablo!
PAAABLOOO!
INTRUDERS!

The heroes froze in panic. The momentary silence was broken by the THUD, THUD, THUD of a golem clunking down a set of stairs. It appeared in the doorway.

PABLO CLEANING MASTER'S TOILET. INTRUDERS NO WELCOME.

When it looked as though Hoofius was cornered with nowhere to run, the cage Twinkle was untying came crashing down.

As it slammed against the golem's head, the door opened and Chompy tumbled out onto the floor. Twinkle had to pull him to safety as Pablo staggered around the room, confused.

'OUCH . . . BUMP ON HEAD. . . PABLO DIZZY
. . . INITIATING SLEEPY MODE . . .'

The golem keeled over with an almighty
THUNK.

A-ha!
A fine
victory!

'How dare you!' came a voice from the doorway—the same wizard they saw in the mirror—Frederico Four-hats. 'Breaking into a grand wizard's tower? Trying on his clothes? Vandalizing his golem? Freeing his prisoner? I'm afraid that is all punishable by Wizard City law.'

'You can't have Chompy!' said Twinkle. Thinking quickly, she ushered him out of the window, away from the wizard. 'We'll come and find you!' she called as the gargoyle glided out and away.

Frederico didn't seem bothered in the slightest.

It was the heroes that he wanted.

CHAPTER TEN

PRISON BREAK

The next few moments passed in a blur, and seemed to end with cries of 'oof!' and 'argh!' as Hoofius, Twinkle, and Trevor found themselves landing in a heap on a cold, hard floor.

> Hey! I just swept that floor!

They looked up in the direction of a familiar voice.

GNOMEDALF!

'Where are we? What's going on?' said a very dazed and confused Hoofius.

'You were sent through a portal, to wizard prison. Herbert is here, too. A master of portal magic can create gateways to wherever they wish. And it seems Frederico Four-hats has got us right where he wants us—trapped in this prison!'

'Not all of us,' said Twinkle. 'Blossom is still on the outside.'

But she had spoken too soon.

Ooof!

'Looks like we're all together again,' said Gnomedalf, picking up a waffle and taking a bite. 'At least this beats prison food.'

The heroes chewed at waffles as they exchanged stories of how they ended up in Wizard Prison. While Herbert wowed and worried them with his discovery of the secret room and the summoning stone, he was just as keen to hear about the golem chase and Chompy's rescue. Then came Blossom's turn.

He was out on a waffle delivery to a fancy tower when . . .

Come in!

KNOCK
KNOCK

'So, Frederico plans to summon the Mega Gargoyle during the Great Wizard Bake-tacular tomorrow, when the wizards will have left their staffs at home and be unable to stop him,' said Gnomedalf. 'And neither will we.'

Strips of flowing pink energy prevented any escape from their cell.

'Don't lick that!' Gnomedalf warned, as Blossom went in for a taste. Pink *usually* meant sweet and delicious.

What did I tell you?

'The magical energy only harms living things. It allows the guard golems to move about freely, as they are manufactured beings. It's quite genius, really,' said Herbert, as Blossom nursed his tongue.

'Then, that's it? we've failed the quest?' asked Hoofius.

'I'm afraid so,' said Gnomedalf. 'Make yourselves comfortable. We might be here for a very long time.'

'Not if Frederico summons the Mega Gargoyle tomorrow and it destroys the entire city,' said Blossom unhelpfully.

As the night drew in, the heroes sat and glumly pondered their fate until the lights went out.

After a less than comfortable night on the hard floors of wizard prison, the heroes awoke to the rattling sound of a golem wheeling a breakfast trolley into their cell. Gnomedalf rubbed his sleepy eyes in disbelief.

BETSY? Is that you? It's me, Gnomedalf!

SSHHH THIS IS A PRISON.

'How could she forget me?' sobbed the old gnome as Betsy continued her rounds.

'BLEH!' spluttered Blossom as he sampled the prison food. 'Couldn't you ask the golem to bring some candy floss and a few cream buns? Maybe a hot chocolate to wash it all down?'

'I'm not her master anymore!' wailed Gnomedalf, before coming to a sudden realization. 'Of course! I'm not her master. We need to change her master key!'

The others all looked at each other in puzzlement.

'Master keys are like a golem's memory. Every bit of information a golem learns is imprinted onto it. If you change the key, then the golem's memory has to start all over again. We just need to put my master key back in!'

'But where are we going to find that?' asked Hoofius.

Gnomedalf chuckled. 'I kept it on me all these years . . .'

I always wondered what was under there.

When Betsy came back for the empty plates, Blossom hooked his horn through the master key handle in her back and pulled it loose. Twinkle was on hand to slot Gnomedalf's key in and give it a turn.

They each held their breath for a few moments, hoping the magic of the master key would unlock the old Betsy.

'Betsy? *BETSY?*' urged Gnomedalf, desperate for a different response from the golem.

'SHHHHH.' boomed the golem. Their hearts sank to the prison floor.

'BETSY HEARD YOU THE FIRST TIME, MASTER.'

'Ah-ha! She's back!' cried Gnomedalf,

breaking into a jig of excitement. 'And she still has that dead-pan golem wit.'

At Gnomedalf's instruction, Betsy lay down over the magical barrier, blocking its upward flow, and the heroes all clambered over and out, much to the envy of other prisoners.

Together, the heroes hurried to the exit.

'STOP. PRISONERS NO ESCAPE. THIS BEHAVIOUR IS UNSATISFACTORY.' A golem guard was bounding after them and getting closer every second.

'I'm not going to make it!' puffed Gnomedalf, behind the others.

Betsy turned and crashed into the onrushing golem. 'MASTER AND FRIENDS ESCAPE. BETSY TAKE CARE OF EVERYTHING.'

Hoofius pulled Gnomedalf through the door to safety as the golems grappled behind them.

They were free.

CHAPTER ELEVEN
THE SHOW-STOPPER

'Oh no! The Bake-tacular is beginning!' cried Gnomedalf, as a bell tower chimed out the eleventh hour of the morning. 'To the Arcanium, with all haste!'

'But what about Chompy?' cried Twinkle. 'I said we would come find him.'

'I'm afraid we have bigger gargoyles to worry about now,' said Gnomedalf, regretfully. Twinkle knew he was right.

They rushed through the streets, not stopping to enjoy the festival atmosphere of a city celebrating its beloved baking competition. The corridors of the Arcanium twisted towards the Grand Hall, where the event had already begun. As they got closer, a commotion echoed down the hall.

Blossom used his horn to part the oncoming wave of wizards, while the others followed behind, and they pushed slowly toward the Grand Hall.

Meanwhile, Frederico stood centre stage, the summoning stone in his hand. He had snuck his wizard staff into the hall, too, and seemed to be enjoying the chaos he was creating.

Ah-haha! Time to whip up your devastation!

Rows of seats emptied all around him, as competing wizards cowered behind their worktops. Only the Wizard Supreme, Barnabus Five-hats, stood his ground.

'This is madness, Frederico!' boomed Barnabus, as he kept a nervous distance from the rogue wizard. 'Why!? Why are you doing this?'

Frederico's face flared in anger. 'Because I've never won the Bake-tacular, and it's all your fault! You are not a fair judge!'

'Your cakes have soggy bottoms, Frederico. You know this!' replied Barnabus firmly, stepping closer.

But Frederico had heard enough. 'If I can't win, then no one will!'

Frederico turned his attention back to his work. This was the moment he had been preparing for.

'I, Frederico, have mastered portal magic like no other. I have summoned beasts far and wide to this world. And now only one more remains. The beast that will command them all but answer only to ME!'

He began waving his staff, the air bending and swirling above his head, expanding to an enormous size. A portal. Thunder boomed and bolts of lightning lit up from inside it.

Frederico held up the summoning stone and spoke a series of secret words. The stone burned with a blue flame, although the wizard wasn't harmed. A few moments passed, and then a shadow loomed from within.

'BEHOLD THE ULTIMATE SHOW-STOPPER!' cried Frederico, above the boom and sound of fleeing wizards.

'No . . . we're too late!' stammered Gnomedalf, as he and the others finally fought their way into the hall. The sight of the Mega Gargoyle stunned them to the spot. With the stone in his hand, the colossal beast was under Frederico's control.

'Now, Mega Gargoyle. Call out to the others that came before you! Lure them to Wizard City!'

The gargoyle threw back its head and let out a deafening roar.

Barnabus could barely keep his toppings in place.

Across the land, the gargoyles that Frederico had summoned in the days and weeks before heeded the call.

An army began to gather.

Frederico grinned maniacally at the sight of the power he commanded. But the uproar of the Mega Gargoyle made the room shake. The empty stacks of pots and pans behind Frederico—that would have been filled with batter and cake mix—began to wobble.

He noticed a moment too late.

AHHHH!

The summoning stone fell from Frederico's hands and rolled away, as he was buried beneath a wave of baking equipment.

'Now!' yelled Barnabus. 'Take the stone! Send the beast back!'

Hoofius reached for the summoning stone, but the shadow of the Mega Gargoyle's foot made him leap backwards. It crushed the stone to dust and let out a triumphant roar.

With no one to answer to, it beat its wings and took to the air, crashing through the Arcanium wall and into the city.

They all stared in disbelief at the gaping hole in the wall, as more and more gargoyles filled the sky beyond.

'Look at all those gargoyles,' said Trevor. 'Frederico was certainly busy.'

'So, that's it. We're all doomed,' mourned Hoofius.

'It's not all bad,' said Blossom, picking up Barnabus.

'At least we have cake!'

HEY!

CHAPTER TWELVE
MEGA PROBLEMS

Outside, the Mega Gargoyle was wrecking havoc across Wizard City, as other gargoyles joined in the fun.

Do you mind? I am TRYING to study!

The apprentice wizards stood no chance.

Hocus kadabra! Err... abra pocus? No that's not it. Uh-oh.

Back in the Arcanium, the heroes were desperately trying to form a plan.

'Can you please tell your friend to stop eating me?' begged Cake Barnabus.

'Eating helps me think,' said Blossom, popping another cherry into his mouth.

'An irresistible treat . . .' thought Herbert aloud. 'That might just do it!'

Gnomedalf cottoned on to his friend's plan. 'Of course . . . you lured Chompy into my kitchen cupboard with a waffle. We could try and lure the Mega Gargoyle back into the portal!'

'We'd need something bigger and tastier than Barnabus for that,' added Trevor.

Blossom suddenly had an idea so brilliant that he dropped the wizard cake on the floor in disbelief.

'Leave it to me!'

Blossom raced out of the Arcanium and through Wizard City, with Twinkle fluttering beside him. They didn't exactly look out of place—the streets were full of panic—and they dodged their way through gargoyles and the blasts of magical energy from wizards trying to fight back.

But there was one wizard in particular that they were looking for.

WHIZZPOP'S
WAFFLE
WAGON

TRY MY WAFFLES
They're magic!

'Whizzpop, it's me!' cried Blossom above the din. 'We need your help!'

But Whizzpop seemed no happier to see Blossom than he did the gargoyles.

'Well, well, well! If it isn't the worst waffle deliverer in Wizard City. You're fired!'

'It's not my fault I didn't come back, I was in prison!' cried Blossom. As excuses went, it didn't sound the most believable. 'We need your help to stop the gargoyles or we'll all be doomed!'

The cry of the Mega Gargoyle from nearby shook the city, making Whizzpop jump in alarm. 'OK . . . I'm listening.'

Blossom explained his idea, as the gargoyles flew off to the rallying cry of their superior.

'You want a GIANT waffle?' said the wizard. 'Do you know how hard I'd have to click my fingers to conjure one that big?'

'*Pleeease!*' begged Twinkle. 'You can do it!'

Whizzpop grabbed his staff and concentrated all his power into his magic fingers.

Here I go! My biggest, fluffiest, tastiest waffle ever! There ain't no waffle like a . . . . . . WHIZZPOP WAFFLE!

A massive waffle appeared and flumped to the ground in front of them.

'Wow! It's so light!' said Twinkle, throwing it up in the air. It flipped over and floated gently back into her palms.

'And tasty!' said Blossom, tearing off a piece and filling his mouth.

'What did I tell you? My waffles are magic!' Whizzpop beamed. 'But you'd better get outta here before those gargoyles come back!'

Twinkle flew towards the Arcanium with the giant waffle in her hands and the fate of the world on her shoulders.

The smell of the waffle sent the gargoyles into a craze, as they shrieked and chased her through the sky. But Twinkle had no time to look behind.

As her friends below cheered her on, she hauled the oversized waffle through the battered hole in the Arcanium wall. The portal whirled in front of her, but the thunder from within was drowned out by the swarm of gnashing teeth and claws as the gargoyles poured in after her.

Twinkle took a breath, and heaved the waffle into the void.

Twinkle's voice snapped Chompy out of the frenzy he was caught up in. But just as he turned towards her, he got knocked to the ground by the rush for the waffle.

As the last of the gargoyles disappeared into the portal, a roar erupted from outside. The beating of giant wings got closer. The Mega Gargoyle was here.

'It's in there!' yelled Twinkle, hoping it hadn't lost the scent. 'And it's delicious.' She rubbed her stomach and licked her lips, trying to encourage the beast through the portal.

But the Mega Gargoyle wasn't fooled. It wanted revenge for losing its army.

It wanted Twinkle.

'TWINKLE!' cried Hoofius. Her friends could only watch helplessly from the floor.

The beast raised its mighty arm to swipe and roared again in fury.

Ewww! Gargoyle breath!

It hesitated. Something blurred in front of its eyes.

It landed on the Mega Gargoyle's nose.

And it took a bite.

The giant beast yowled as it tried to flick him off. But Chompy was too fast. He landed again and took another bite.

'Ooof. I know how that feels,' said Trevor, as Chompy sunk his teeth in again.

RRGHH

The beast spun around again and again, trying to swat at Chompy. And then with one last, dizzy lunge at the lesser gargoyle, it was gone.

Barnabus wasn't taking any chances.

'Now, Gnomedalf! Use the staff . . . close the portal!'

The gnome picked up Frederico's staff, and his wizard days came rushing back.

Wah-ho! Much more fun than a broom!

The portal began to shrink, and the sounds of gargoyles, thunder, and lightning became more and more distant. Moments later, it was as if it had never even been there.

CHAPTER THIRTEEN
PANIC OVER

'Is everyone OK?' said Hoofius, breaking the quiet.

'Well, I'm still a cake,' said Barnabus. 'But one can't complain too much.'

Around them wizards were coming out of hiding and dusting themselves down. Timothy Two-hats hopped out from under a pudding bowl. He took one look at Barnabus and burst into a fit of croaky frog giggles.

Gnomedalf wiped his brow and set down
Frederico's staff. It was still pulsing
with magical power. 'That's quite enough
excitement for me.'

'I am sorry I ever doubted you, Gnomedalf,'
said Barnabus, a jammy tear forming
under his eye. 'I was fooled by Frederico's

tricks. He must have enchanted your rolling pin, to gain an advantage from your banishment. Well, he may have taken your place on the council, but his cakes were still terrible!'

There was a groan from nearby as Frederico crawled out from under the heap of pans, nursing a bump on the head.

On realizing the failure of his plan, he staggered to his feet and made a run for the door.

I'm not finished yet! I'll show you all!

As the rogue wizard was about to disappear, he slammed face first into something hard and heavy coming round the corner.

'That won't be necessary!' said Gnomedalf, patting his old golem on the arm. 'Though

I'm sure we could use your help in escorting Mr Four-Hats to his new home.'

'What happened? Is it all over?' asked Blossom, as he and Whizzpop stepped out from behind the golem.

'It's over, thanks to you all. But especially our gargoyle friend,' said Gnomedalf.

Twinkle was giving Chompy quite the squeeze.

YOU SAVED
US ALL!

Chompy welcomed the hugs, before the sight and smell of Cake Barnabus caught his attention.

'If I may . . .' interrupted Gnomedalf.

'Don't you heroes usually have a way of celebrating a completed quest? I would hate to miss out on my one opportunity . . .'

He wasn't alone.

So long! Remember to tell your friends about Whizzpop's waffles. They're MAGIC!

croak

'Farewell, Gnomedalf Four-hats!' called Barnabus, as the heroes set out on the road home. 'You and your friends are always welcome, and a place on the Grand Wizard Council will forever be open to you!'

Twinkle turned and flew back to Chompy. One last hug wouldn't hurt.

'I'm sorry you can't come with us,' said Twinkle, with a sniff. 'But our quest was to take you to the wizards. And now they know what a hero you are. This is your home now.'

'Hey, don't worry about a thing. I'll take good care of him,' assured Whizzpop. He clicked his fingers and a waffle appeared. He tore a chunk off and handed it to Chompy. 'Maybe I'll even tame him.'

Chompy let out a burp.

'I wouldn't count on it,' said Twinkle. 'Goodbye Chompy. You're not a lesser gargoyle to me.'

The heroes walked wearily away as the towers and spires shrank into the distance.

'I do enjoy a city break!' said Herbert, thumbing through his guidebook. 'Hmm. They may need to rewrite some of this, though. The Arcanium has a big hole in it now. And there are fewer spires . . .'

'Gnomedalf, how come you didn't want to stay and be a wizard again?' asked Blossom.

The old gnome chuckled, his broom back in his hand. 'Being a wizard is too much hard work! Plus, starting today, I may even get to put my feet up a bit more often . . .'

The clunk of heavy steps sounded behind as Betsy caught them up.

How did I ever manage without you?

As the heroes at last arrived back home to the Super Happy Magic Forest, a big crowd had gathered.

'Ho-ho! Yes! Hello one and all! We're back again!' cried Gnomedalf, waving at everyone, to little fanfare. But it seemed the crowd wasn't gathered for them.

Something large and furry was stealing the show. And sitting atop it was the Wood Elf Queen..

FORGETTING SOMETHING?

The Council of Happiness was there, too. Tiddlywink saw the heroes and marched straight up to them. His face was the usual shade of ripe tomato.

'What's going on here? Why is there a smelly MOOSE rampaging through the forest? And what's THIS thing?'

Tiddlywink gave Betsy a kick and then regretted it.

Owww.

'Strawberry is smelly because he rolled in yucky mud!' said the Wood Elf Queen, as Tiddlywink hopped around like a bunny.

'And he ruined his beautiful makeover.
Didn't you, Strawberry?'

The moose moaned.

'Your hero friends owe me a favour. And I
want them to clean my mucky moose from
head to hoof!'

'Not quite the homecoming I imagined,'
whispered Trevor to the others.

The heroes looked to Nym, who shrugged
her shoulders apologetically. There would
be no getting out of this one.

With the quest complete, there really was
only one thing left to do . . .

As peace returned to the land and Wizard City, Maggie Three-hats was tasked with finding a spell that could turn Timothy and Barnabus back.

Chompy delivered Whizzpop's Waffles all over Wizard City.

And enjoyed all the perks the job had to offer.

Have you seen those free samples?

While Frederico was set to work in the Wizard Prison Laundry room.

Darn these spaghetti stains!

Back in the Super Happy Magic Forest,
Herbert helped Trevor re-grow his head.

Betsy was a bit too big for Gnomedalf's house . . .

. . . but there was plenty of room in the garden.

MATTY LONG

As a young boy Matty always thought he would grow up to be a game show host. But instead he became the next best thing: an illustrator and author! He has mostly made picture books and this is his first chapter book so he hopes you like it and want to tell everyone.

When Matty is not working, he's usually telling himself he should be working. All while playing video games.

Matty lives in Ely, Cambridgeshire and still doesn't have a cat.

You can find him online at www.mattylong.com

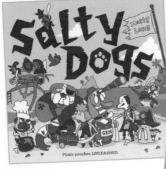